VALLEY COTTAGE FREE LIBRARY
W9-BBP-124
May 2015

VALLEY COTTAGE LIBRARY
110 Route 303
Valley Cottage, NY
10989
www.vclib.org

Stanley & Me

Misty

BY CHRISTINE DENCER

ILLUSTRATED BY JESSICA MESERVE

For Mum & Dad
and for Erin. –C.D.

For the children at Highbury
School in Hitchin. —J.M.

Published in 2014 by Simply Read Books www.simplyreadbooks.com

Library and Archives Canada Cataloguing in Publication

Dencer, Christine, author
Misty / written by Christine Dencer ; illustrated by Jessica
Meserve.

(Stanley & me)
ISBN 978-1-927018-59-0 (bound)

I. Meserve, Jessica, illustrator II. Title.

PS8607.E597M57 2014 jC813'.6 C2014-900439-7

We gratefully acknowledge for their financial support of our publishing program the Canada Council for the Arts, the BC Arts Council, and the Government of Canada through the Canada Book Fund (CBF).

Manufactured in Malaysia.

Book design by Sara Gillingham Studio.

10 9 8 7 6 5 4 3 2 1

CONTENTS

Chapter 1

MISTY WANTS TO PLAY p5

Chapter 2

A VERY IMPORTANT JOB p10

Chapter 3

I AM AFRAID p16

Chapter 4

BEING BRAVE p22

Chapter 1

MISTY WANTS TO PLAY

Stanley is my best friend. He lives in the house across the street.

I play with Stanley in my front yard every day after school. But we did not always play in my yard. We used to play in the big bush in Stanley's yard. Then Stanley got a dog.

Every day, Stanley asks, “Do you want to play in my yard today?”

Every day, I say, “No, thanks.”

I would like to play
in Stanley's yard, but
I am afraid of his dog.

Stanley's dog is big and black. Her name is Misty. She sits outside tied to a long rope.

When Stanley and I play in
my front yard, Misty runs and
jumps and barks.

“Misty says she wants to play
with us,” says Stanley.

I do not know what Misty says.
I do not speak Woof.

Chapter 2
A VERY IMPORTANT JOB

Stanley is not at school today.

“Stanley hurt his arm,” says Mrs. Green. “Let’s make him a get-well card.”

We all work together to make a get-well card for Stanley. I draw a picture of Stanley and me and Misty playing together in Stanley’s yard.

"Who will take the card to Stanley?" asks Mrs. Green.

I jump up and say, "I will!"

"It is a very important job," says Mrs. Green.

"I can do it," I say.

Then I remember Misty. I will have to go to Stanley's house to take the card to him, but I am afraid of Misty. I am about to say that I have piano lessons after

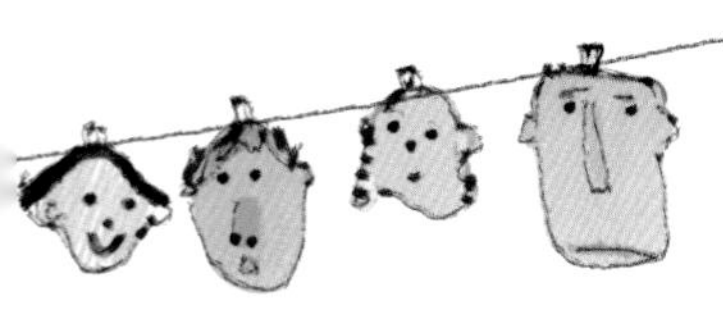

school, when Mrs. Green says, “That’s wonderful, Sophie. Thank you.”

Chapter 3

I AM AFRAID

So here I sit on my front steps. Misty sits at the end of her long rope across the street at Stanley's house.

"Where is Stanley?" I call.

Misty wags her tail. "Woof!" she says.

I do not understand.

“Can I come over?”

Misty jumps up.
“Woof!” she says.

I do not understand if
she means yes or no.

Then the front window opens
and I see Stanley's face.

"Hi, Sophie," he calls.

"Hi, Stanley! Is your arm better?"

"A little better," he says.
"What are you doing?"

"I have a card for you," I say.

"Are you going to bring it to me?"

"I want to, but I am afraid of Misty."

"She is a nice dog," says Stanley.

"She is big."

"Yes. She is big," says Stanley.
"But she is a nice dog."

"She jumps."

"Tell her to sit and stay," says Stanley.

"I do not speak Woof."

"It's okay. Misty speaks People," says Stanley.

"I am afraid," I whisper.

"You can do it,
Sophie!" says
Stanley.

Chapter 4

BEING BRAVE

I feel like crying. I look at the card in my hand. I see the picture I drew of Stanley and me and Misty playing together. Then I hear Mrs. Green's voice inside my head saying, “It is a very important job.”

I look across the street and see my best friend. He looks sad.

I take a deep breath and walk across the street.

Misty stands up and jumps and barks.

I stop and I shout, “Misty, sit!”

Misty sits.

When she is sitting, she does not look so big.

I put my hand up and I say, "Misty, stay!"

Misty stays.

I walk up to the front door.

The front door opens. Stanley is smiling so big!

"You did it!" he says.

I am smiling too, but my legs feel wobbly like the Jell-O I ate at lunch.

I give Stanley his card with the picture I drew of him and me and Misty playing together in Stanley's yard.

When it is time to go home, I feel afraid to walk past Misty again but not as afraid as before. I feel better when Stanley's mother wants to walk me across the street.

"In case of cars,"
she says, winking
at me.

I am glad. I have had enough of being brave for one day. But who knows what I can do tomorrow!